TOP SECRET MESSAGE

Hi, I'm M t, and I have a superpower.

Until recently I was just ordinary – going to school, having a laugh with my mates, liking a girl called Emma who liked me too – but as a friend. I wanted it to be more.

Then, one fateful day, I visited an old lady ca led Mrs Jameson. She was supposed to be ve y difficult and didn't get along with anyone. Ex ept, would you believe, me. Soon I was v iting her every day and when she died she le me a crystal, which she had always worn a und her neck.

There was a note from her too, saying no o else can ever know how special the crystal is Only me.

And one day I discovered the crystal's incredible power.

IT CAN READ MINDS …

MindReader

GHOSTLY WHISPER

Pete Johnson

award

ISBN 978-1-78270-305-1

Cover design by Patrick Knowles
Illustration by Anthony Smith

First published by Award Publications Limited 2018

Published by Award Publications Limited,
The Old Riding School, Welbeck, Worksop, S80 3LR

www.awardpublications.co.uk

18 1

Printed in the United Kingdom

*This book is dedicated, with huge admiration,
to my favourite Golden Age detective writers:
Agatha Christie, Josephine Tey
and Patricia Moyes.*

Chapter One

Night-time Tumble

Yes, I know I told you Emma only liked me as a friend. But things were changing between us. She hadn't said anything, but there was something in the air. I sensed it.

Now was definitely the moment to ask Emma out.

Only, I could be wrong. It would be beyond horrible if she shuddered and said, "No way." So why didn't I check out how she felt about me with my crystal?

I did think about doing that. But I'd already decided tuning in to friends was a bit sneaky.

Well it is, isn't it?

So I picked the moment I'd take a chance and ask Emma out.

I chose a weekend near the end of term – and Christmas.

Emma had been away but was returning on Sunday afternoon. And after tea we were meeting up – as we often did – to take our dogs for a walk. We were always especially relaxed then, so it seemed like the perfect time.

But at the very last moment, our plans were changed.

Emma rang me and asked, "Could you do me a massive favour?"

"Sure, just name it."

"It's about Finn."

Finn is, without doubt, the biggest show-off to walk this earth. And it was bad enough having to endure him at school – I certainly didn't want to waste a precious second talking about him now.

"What about him?" I asked very cautiously.

I could hear Emma take a deep breath before saying quickly, "The thing is, Finn's mum has turned her garden shed into a den, just for him. And he keeps on and on at me to go and see it."

"Just say no."

"I so want to — but, well, I thought if you came with me we could pop in and out dead fast."

"How fast?" I demanded.

"Ten minutes — tops."

"Make it nine."

"OK."

"Eight would be even better."

She laughed. "This is so good of you, Matt."

"I know."

"Then I promise we'll escape and take Bess and Scampi out and have a brilliant evening."

So at half past six, Emma and I trudged up the gravel drive to Finn's mansion. His mum opened the door and announced, "He's waiting for you," as if we were about to be granted an audience with a young emperor. "He is with his cousin, Martyn, and Martyn's brought his dog, Percy, with him."

"We like dogs," said Emma.

"It's only Finn we hate," I whispered. Emma

smothered a laugh.

Finn's mum opened the back gate. "Please follow me, but be careful, as it's so dark tonight, and isn't it cold?" Before we could reply, she'd moved on to her all-time favourite subject – Finn. "Poor Finn gets so stressed sometimes – his artistic temperament, of course. He needs somewhere quiet and calm, a space all of his own, and now he has it – Finn's den." She pointed proudly.

Finn's den was approximately one thousand times bigger than the shed lurking down at the bottom of my garden, which is a big hit with all the local spiders. In fact, it's like their community centre but otherwise it's just a rest home for decaying plant pots. While Finn's was … I was seething with envy already and I hadn't even stepped inside it.

Then we heard Finn's unmistakable tones. "I won! I've won again!" He hurtled out of his den with a huge smirk stuck to his face. He was followed by a smallish boy with spiky hair and a very large dog.

"What have you won, love?" asked his mum.

"Table football — four games in a row. How do I do it?" He grinned at Emma before viewing me considerably less enthusiastically.

"Well, I'll leave you all to have fun," said Finn's mum. "And don't forget, we have prizes for you all."

"Prizes?" cried Emma.

"Tell you about it later," said Finn. "But first let me show you round my den."

And he did. We saw the table football, the plump, extremely comfortable looking sofa, the fridge, his marvellous internet connection, so he could use his shiny new smartphone whenever he wanted ...

"You could live here for days," said Emma.

Finn nodded, bursting with pride, and then looked at me expectantly. "Yeah, this is such a great ..." I paused, "... playroom."

"Playroom," spluttered Finn. "What are you talking about, Spud?" Finn is the only person still to call me by my old nickname.

Before I could reply, Emma cut in. "I want to hear more about these prizes."

"We have some top prizes — extremely

expensive, aren't they?" Finn looked at Martyn. He nodded enthusiastically and said, "But you gotta earn them though, doing some dead easy challenges."

I looked at my watch. "We can't stay much longer."

"You'd better do your challenge now then," said Finn. And a look passed between him and Martyn. The next moment, Finn was handing me an envelope.

"Wow, it's even got my name on it, what an honour." I ripped it open and read aloud:

MATT, YOU MUST FIND YOUR PRIZE IN THE GARDEN IN THREE MINUTES. IF YOU FAIL TO DO THIS YOU WILL LOSE YOUR PRIZE AND HAVE TO DO A FORFEIT.

"Three minutes isn't very long!" cried Emma. "It could be anywhere."

"He can have longer if he really wants," said Finn grudgingly. "But it's not hard to find, is it?" He turned to Martyn. He was clearly Finn's fanboy and agreed. "It's in an incredibly obvious place."

"You could at least give Matt a clue," persisted Emma.

But I didn't need a clue. Not when I had a superpower. And I'd use it now to put Finn in his place. I quickly tilted my crystal towards Finn, impatient for it to get warm. "So I'll be able to find it in three minutes?" I asked.

"I could find it in one minute, couldn't I?" said Finn.

His fanboy nodded.

"And you say it's somewhere dead obvious?" I asked.

"It really is." Finn smiled, but I 'overheard':

But Spud'll never think of looking through the bin where we keep all the magazines and paper. And he'll be humiliated in front of Emma. It's going to be epic.

I grinned to myself and then jumped up so quickly, Percy gave a bark of alarm.

"Right, let's do this," I announced, eager to

get started.

"I still think you should have at least one clue," cried Emma.

"No, it's not necessary." Do you know, my voice actually deepened as I said that, and I did a kind of glide strut to the shed door.

I could picture it all. I'd find the prize in well under three minutes, ask out a hugely impressed Emma and – well, we'd live happily ever after, wouldn't we? The End.

"I'll see you all in three minutes then," I said, "and probably sooner." I tell you, right then I wasn't cool – I was super cool.

"Best of luck, Matt," said Emma with a big smile, which made me feel great.

"Your time starts now," announced Finn.

Outside, it hit me how dark it was. In fact, the darkness tonight was so thick you practically had to wade through it. And the torch, which I'd promised Mum I'd take with me tonight, was … well, it wasn't in my coat pocket anyway.

What should I do? Go back to the shed and get a torch. That seemed more than a bit feeble.

Besides, I was sure my eyes would get used to the darkness soon. I only had to wait a few seconds.

So I waited. It wasn't much better, but definitely too late to go back now. Still, I have a pretty good sense of direction so I began to edge forward. I was sure I was moving in the direction of the back gate where all the bins were kept. I was sure I could still do this.

Out of the darkness, I suddenly heard Finn shout. "Two minutes gone, just one minute left." He couldn't have sounded more triumphant. I really had to move fast. I sped forward and immediately slammed into something so hard and painful it sent me flying backwards. And it was so unexpected. I couldn't save myself and toppled on to the ground.

I peered around and now I could make out what had ambushed me. A large garden seat had been waiting silently and sneakily in the dark. And it had sent me reeling into all this thick mud. I was absolutely covered in the stuff.

Then I sniffed deeply and nearly threw up

with horror. I'd tumbled into a massive pile of dog poo.

Chapter Two

Stinky

The next thing I knew, Finn was yelling, "Time's up!" and thundering across the garden – he never moved this fast during cross-country. Before I could get up, his torch glimmered ghostly white over me.

Finn couldn't speak at first – he was too busy laughing. Martyn took one look at me and also doubled over in side-splitting laughter, and if dogs could laugh, I'm sure Percy would have joined in too.

Everyone was having a fabulous time – except me. I pushed myself to my feet. At once

Finn yelled, "You stink! I mean you *really* whiff!"

And Martyn started doing this fake coughing. I don't know who was more annoying. I just know I've never felt so stupid. You'd never guess I was a boy with a superpower.

If only I could turn back time – I'd give anything to replay the last few minutes although I'd settle for being able to zap a death ray in Finn and Martyn's direction. Then Emma rushed over.

"Look at him. Look at him," yelled Finn. "But don't get too close, the smell might knock you out."

I hated Emma seeing me like that. But at least hers was a friendly face, someone to be on my side. So you won't believe what I'm going to tell you next.

Emma laughed.

OK, it was only for a couple of seconds. More of a snigger really, but I was still shocked by her total disloyalty.

She quickly tried to recover and said softly, "Poor Matt, you've had a bit of an accident then." But I didn't want her pity either.

"What on earth are you all doing?" Finn's mother appeared, waving yet another torch.

"Matt's fallen into a massive pile of dog poo," shouted Finn.

"Oh no," cried Finn's mum. "You really should have cleaned up the garden before your guests arrived, Finn. It's your responsibility." But not even a rare rebuke from his mum could dent Finn's good mood.

His mum approached me very cautiously, as if I was suddenly going to explode or something. "I think it would be best, dear, if you come inside with me now and have a nice bath."

"Have a nice bath!" Finn exploded into laughter again. "Yeah, off you go now, like a good little boy."

"Thanks for the offer," I said to Finn's mum, "but I'm going home."

"You've got to do a double forfeit first," said Finn.

"I'm going home," I repeated firmly.

"I'll come with you," said Emma.

I faced her. "I'd rather be on my own, actually."

Emma flinched. Good.

"Make sure you go straight home, dear," called Finn's mum after me.

"And have a good bath!" shouted Finn.

"Bye, Stinky!" yelled Martyn. That little pipsqueak making fun of me. I bet he goes to sleep in a slipper. But I showed iron self-control and didn't look back once.

And I couldn't go home yet. Too upset, never mind all that washing I was going to have to do. Besides, if I walked about for a bit, maybe the stink would start dropping off me. (It didn't.)

I'd had such big plans for tonight. And instead … Emma had actually laughed at me with Finn and his little fanboy. And then, after behaving so treacherously, she thought we were going to stroll away together.

I still had some pride left.

Wandering around the parade of shops I knew so well, a guy of about eighteen stomped towards me, totally lost in thought. But about what?

I had the power to find out and tilted my crystal in his direction.

So I've been overlooked for the football squad again. Just a reserve. They didn't give me a chance.

As he trudged past I said, "I never get picked for the football team either."

He actually stopped. "What did you just say?" he croaked.

"Laters." I grinned, and darted quickly away from him. When I looked round, he was still standing there shaking his head.

That was fun. Who should I eavesdrop on next? I picked a guy, moving swiftly down the road, head lowered, thinking deeply about something.

Only I could find out what it was. And that's when I received the shock of my life.

Chapter Three

"In danger every second"

I've listened in to tons of people. No, not tons, that makes me sound dead nosy. But anyway, quite a few, and I tell you, I've never heard a voice before like this one. It sounded so desperate and scared and bitter. And I didn't like it at all.

This is what I overheard:

All right, I'll turn up at three tomorrow and do what they want. Got no choice. But I've told them I'm not staying on after Friday night. I'm in danger every second at Fairview.

That last sentence so stunned me I let out a gasp of shock, just as he passed by me as well. No wonder he turned round, and for a moment the street light illuminated his face – quite young, with a swirl of blond hair and wearing the chunkiest black glasses I'd ever seen.

He looked at me, frowned and then strode away just as my mobile went off. It was my mum. She'd been nattering to Finn's mum. Had I hurt myself? Was I sure? And why wasn't I at home?

She sounded quite concerned. I sort of liked that. But blabbermouth Mum not only told Dad about my unfortunate tumble but Alison and her boyfriend as well. So they were all waiting in the doorway for me. Alison immediately fell about laughing, holding her nose and saying she needed a mask. And soon all four of them were rocking with laughter.

Only my dog, Scampi, showed me any sympathy, and sat gravely watching me do something highly unusual – take a shower.

But all that time and later in bed, I still kept thinking about that desperate voice saying how he was in danger every second at Fairview.

In danger! From who or what?

And where was Fairview, anyway? Could it be the name of a house?

I casually mentioned it to Mum when she popped into my bedroom and she said at once, "Oh yes, that's where Mrs Prentice lives – she and I ran a stall at the local jumble sale recently. Very nice woman – if a bit scatty."

"And do you know where Fairview is?" I asked.

"Yes, I've been there for coffee. It's off a lane near where your friend Finn lives."

"Mum, he is not my friend. So who else lives there?"

"Her husband and her son – what's his name, Artie. But he's away at school at the moment."

"And that's all?" I asked.

"Yes, I think so."

"They're not expecting anyone else – like a guest or lodger?"

"I don't think so." Mum looked puzzled. "Why?"

"I just wondered, that's all," I said, and I

legged it before she could ask me any questions.

After Mum left, I wondered some more. It would be sort of fascinating to see if that guy I'd overheard did turn up at Fairview tomorrow.

Maybe I should think up some reason to roll up there tomorrow and find out.

But what if that guy in the thick glasses really was there – and remembered me?

Unlikely. He only saw me for a second. And anyway, what if he did?

He's quite unaware I know.

What exactly do I know ...?

Chapter Four

Running Away

Usually Emma and I walk to school together, chattering away the whole time. Today, though, there was an embarrassed silence when we first saw each other, broken by me snapping, "Enjoy yourself last night, did you?"

"Of course not," she snapped back. "And I thought the whole point of you coming round was so we could escape from Finn's house together. Instead, you go off in a right strop — and leave me there."

"Are you surprised?"

"You fell over into a bit of dog poo. So what?"

"You made it far, far worse," I said.

She stopped walking. "I did? How?"

"By laughing."

Emma shook her head. "I never laughed."

"You so did," I cried.

She hesitated. "Might have grinned, that's all. It was sort of funny."

"I've had nightmares that were funnier. You let me down last night."

"No, you let me down."

We didn't say another word to each other.

At school, though, something was going on and Finn was right in the centre of it. Then I noticed how everyone kept looking at me and laughing. So Finn was telling everyone about my escapade last night. I'd expected that.

But I hadn't expected a girl I'd never spoken to before, to come up to me and say, "That picture of you is so dark you can hardly see anything."

Her name was Lucy Chu and she was new to my school. She was also a total brainbox and hadn't made a single friend, as all the girls said she was 'stuck up' and 'loved herself'.

Lucy Chu went on, "So I wouldn't worry about it," in quite a kindly way too. It's just I hadn't a clue what she was talking about.

Then a solemn-looking Emma came over — and Lucy immediately vanished. "What's going on?" I asked.

Emma said, "Finn's cousin took a picture of you on Sunday night when you were ... Well, Finn's sent it to everyone. You might even get it."

I smiled. "So if ever I get big-headed I'll just peek at that cheery snap."

"You can't see much at all," said Emma. "It's very dark."

"That's what Lucy said."

"Lucy Chu actually spoke to you? You are honoured," she added. "I didn't know about the photo. Honestly."

"I believe you," I said at once. I added, "Shall we just forget about last night?" Emma suddenly smiled at me, and my stomach went all wobbly. I really do like her.

"Last night happened in an alternative universe," she said.

That photo was still very much in this universe though. I just laughed it off. It's all you can do, isn't it, and hope people will eventually get bored of going on about it.

Later, in the dining hall, it was Lucy who was getting a hard time from the girls in my year. Again, Nicola yelled at her, "Hey, Lucy, I want to be your friend! No, really I do. So come and talk to me."

But Lucy completely blanked her, causing Nicola to shriek, "Did you see that? She gave me the dirtiest look ever. You really think you're way above us all, don't you?"

Later, I spotted Lucy reading a book in the library. "Hey, thanks for alerting me about that photo," I said. She didn't even look up. Then I noticed she was reading *The ABC Murders* by Agatha Christie.

"That book is ace, by the way," I said. "I've just finished it and you'll never guess the ending."

No reaction at all, she didn't even lower her book. Maybe all the girls in my class were right. Lucy was 'stuck up'.

But she'd tried to warn me about Finn's photo. That wasn't stuck up. Almost without realising it, I started tilting my crystal in Lucy's direction:

I felt sorry for this boy this morning. And I know exactly what it feels like to be picked on. I feel bad not even answering him too. He might be all right. But I can't take that chance. I just want to be invisible.

I stared at her. Was that what she really wanted — to be invisible? That was kind of shocking.

Still, I shan't be here much longer.

Why, where was she going? My crystal became too hot to hold so I had to allow it to cool down before I very impatiently activated it again and picked up:

I'll get up, take my bag, and walk

slowly and casually out of the library, being careful not to attract attention. I'll go to reception, hoping it's as busy and chaotic as it usually is, and quietly slip away, in time to catch the next train to my aunt's house. I've got enough money for the fare too.

I know this was supposed to be my fresh start but it's just as bad as my old school. No one here will care that I'm ...

Then I had to let go of my crystal but I knew the end of that sentence all right.

Lucy was running away.

The next thing I knew, she was walking out of the library. What should I do? Try to stop her? Well I'd better hurry up. So I called across the library.

"Hey, Lucy!"

Very slowly, very warily she turned round. Just about every person in the library was watching us. Now what was I going to say to her?

"Hey, Lucy, just wondered if you'd like to

go somewhere?" What was I talking about? No wonder she blushed red. And so did I, actually.

I struggled to recover. "I wanted to talk to you about—"

"I'm in a hurry," interrupted Lucy, while at the same moment Emma appeared.

She watched Lucy exit quickly from the library and then asked me, "What are you talking to her for?"

"I think she's all right," I said quietly.

"You weren't trying to get her to do your homework, were you?" asked Emma, grinning. "She gets top marks in everything."

"You've discovered my cunning plan." But all the time I was wondering if Lucy had actually left school yet. And a couple of minutes later, I sped into reception but there was no sign of her, so she'd gone. I felt as if I'd let Lucy down.

And I also wondered if I'd ever see her again.

Chapter Five

Getting into Fairview

Actually, I saw Lucy much sooner than I'd expected — in the very next lesson. I was so astonished, I blurted out, "Lucy, you're here. You haven't ..."

"Haven't what?"

"I don't know," I grinned. "I'm talking total rubbish today, aren't I?"

Later, I tuned in to her again:

First thing tomorrow morning I will get registered, then slip away while everyone is going into school assembly. It should be easy then, with so many people surging about. I'll speed off to the railway station and when I'm on the train, I'll text my aunt ...

All at once, I knew exactly what Lucy was doing.

She was daydreaming.

Everyone does it, of course, especially during double maths, but Lucy seemed to spend the whole day imagining herself running away.

Only she won't run away tomorrow morning either, she'll just go on dreaming about it. She must feel incredibly trapped. Not to mention miserable.

And in that moment, I decided I was going to be Lucy's friend — whether she liked it or not.

But first I had to find something I could talk to her about. I knew that she was incredibly clever. But I certainly wasn't, so that was no use. There must be something else.

And that afternoon I overheard:

If I didn't have books I don't know how

I'd get through a day like this. I must get some more Agatha Christie books soon, as I've nearly finished The ABC Murders.

At last, I had the opening I wanted. At the end of school I bounded up and announced, "I've got some Agatha Christie books which you can borrow, if you like."

She looked completely startled. But I quickly added, "It's so good to meet another fan. And by the way, there are no fines if you're late returning them."

She carried on staring at me for a couple of seconds before saying, "OK, thank you."

Lucy had said three whole words to me. Our friendship was really taking off. And straight after school I searched out two Agatha Christie books and left them by my school bag so I wouldn't forget them the next day.

But what of the real-life mystery I'd uncovered? The guy who was in danger every second at Fairview. He belonged in an Agatha Christie book. But instead he was real, so had he actually turned up at the Prentice house?

And could I get into Fairview and find out?

Straight after tea, I took Scampi for his walk as usual, but we went in quite a different direction, running all the way to Finn's house. And then, turning off into a long, winding lane where the houses just got bigger and bigger. Each one had a name, too – not a number.

And there it was, Fairview, with big iron gates that were slightly ajar. So I could wander up the drive, ring on the doorbell and say ... what exactly? Scampi gave a low growl. I thought he was getting impatient but then I realised he'd spotted someone. A boy at the side of the house talking on his mobile.

Could this be Artie – home from boarding school? I bet it was. He was saying, "Can you believe I'm only supposed to use my mobile for an hour a day. I mean, that's nothing, is it? I don't think Mum will give me away, but just in case ..." Scampi gave another low growl.

And all at once I had an idea.

I crouched down and took his lead off. "Scampi, just run around," I hissed. "Run around now." Scampi knew that instruction from our many trips to the park. That meant he could tear about to his heart's content.

And as an extra treat, if no one was at home, I'd say, "Run around now," and Scampi would charge about and even go upstairs (where he's not usually allowed), giving little yelps of delight.

But today Scampi looked puzzled. He knew this wasn't the park or my house. He is so bright.

"Yes, Scampi, it's all right, run around," and I nodded as well.

Not needing any more prompting, Scampi suddenly dived through the gate and started gambolling about, while I ducked out of sight.

Artie spotted Scampi at once. His mobile was hastily thrust away and he raced over to my dog. "Hey, hello there."

Now Scampi is very shy and nervous around strangers. Not surprising because, when he first arrived at the Animal Rescue Centre, he'd been so badly neglected practically all his coat had gone. He needed to be looked after very carefully and I am still the only human he totally trusts. And, although I couldn't hear Scampi's thoughts

with my crystal, he could pick up mine. So I held
the crystal and thought:

It's all right Scampi, he's a friend.

This was a word Scampi knew. So I repeated:

A friend.

Immediately, Scampi stopped jumping about
and let Artie stroke him.

"Aren't you brilliant?" cried Artie. "But
where on earth did you come from?"

Time for me to make an appearance. So up I
popped. "There you are, Scampi," I said, before
adding, "Sorry about that, I only let him off the
lead for a minute."

"No, he's very welcome. You both are."

And by the time I reached them, Scampi was
lying on his back having his tummy vigorously
rubbed by Artie.

"Scampi's really taken to you," I said.

Artie grinned proudly. He was quite small
with dark, curly hair and a cheeky-looking face.

"I'd like to have a dog of my own," he said, "but my dad won't let me as I'm away at boarding school most of the year, worst luck."

"You're Artie, aren't you?"

His smile flickered. "How on earth did you know that?"

"My mum knows your mum."

"My mum's all right except she listens to my dad far too much. He's away right now at a conference in Germany, which I'm really happy about … Hey, how would you and Scampi like to be food tasters?"

"What …"

"I've just made some cakes and need someone to test them. Guaranteed to melt in your mouth – it just might take a day or two," he burst out laughing. "Hey, I know your dog's name – but not yours."

"I'm Matt, and I'd love to try one of your cakes."

"You're very brave, I like that. Come on then. So where do you live?" he added.

"In a house approximately a zillion times smaller than yours. I suppose you need a V.I.P.

pass to get in here."

"Behave," laughed Artie. "But I'll tell you something, Matt – I'd swap it all for a dog like Scampi." And for a moment he looked deadly serious.

And then I was actually inside Fairview. A grandfather clock chimed in the hallway as if to mark the occasion. I'd achieved the first part of my investigation.

Now I just had to find out if that guy I'd overheard had arrived today. But somehow that seemed more and more unlikely. As for the idea of someone being in danger here, well, it almost felt as if I'd dreamt it all last night now.

Artie's mum floated towards me, smiling vaguely as I introduced myself. She said how delighted she was that Artie had found a friend as he gets so lonely during the long holidays. (Artie went bright red when she said that.) After asking me to give my 'dear mum' her very best wishes, she called after me, "I'm afraid you find us in a muddle today."

"She says that every day," grinned Artie. We headed for their sitting room. I took in the log fire crackling in the grate, the well-worn, comfortable armchairs and ...

I stepped back.

Uncurling himself from the biggest chair in the room was a tall man in a crumpled, brown suit.

And he was wearing the thickest glasses you've ever seen.

Chapter Six

A Mystery Solved

As soon as I saw him, my stomach started churning. He really was at Fairview. The place he said he was 'in danger every second'. Only he didn't seem the tiniest bit scared now. And he beamed at Scampi and me, with his very white teeth, as Artie introduced us.

"Mr Travers here," said Artie, "has got the toughest job known to humanity – to try to make me a tiny bit intelligent. No one else in the known universe can do it. That's why I'm bottom of the class in every subject – except cooking, which my dad says doesn't count ..."

"Of course it counts," interrupted Mr Travers. "And you have a rare talent for making delicious cakes, as Matt is about to discover." And very briefly, he peered at me through his amazing glasses.

"By the end of the holiday, Artie," declared Mr Travers, "you might surprise yourself by how much you've improved."

"I doubt it." Artie smiled.

"Anyway, I love a challenge," said Mr Travers. "I've enjoyed meeting you, Matt — and you too of course." He bent down and patted Scampi before breezing out.

Artie immediately confided. "When Dad said I had to have a tutor for the whole Christmas holidays I had a mega meltdown. Especially when I found out that it was someone Dad knew."

I pounced on this. "So how does your dad know him?"

"Oh, he was tutor to the son of some geek Dad does business with. Apparently he worked wonders on his son, who is nearly as thick as me. Then Mr Travers got a job in France, but

Dad heard he was unexpectedly back in Britain staying at some swanky hotel, so he immediately whipped off a letter to Mr Travers – very old school, my dad.

"Only, Dad wasn't expecting him until this weekend, but he's here already – five days early – and we've started working already. Isn't that the most disgusting thing you've heard, Scampi?"

Scampi licked his hand in reply.

"So what's he like?" I asked.

"Too early to say," said Artie. "We've just been chatting and getting to know one another so far – but he keeps blinking at me as if he can't believe how little I know," he chuckled.

It was time to sample Artie's cake. Mr Travers was right. It was delicious. Then I rang Mum to tell her where I was. She was so astonished, she even forgot to remind me it was a school day tomorrow. So I stayed for ages, but Mr Travers didn't return. He'd gone out somewhere. Still, I'd found out plenty.

Later, at home in bed, I struggled to make sense of it all. I had one massive problem. Mr

Travers was two completely different people. Even his voice – all mellow and confident – was nothing like the anxious, scared one I'd picked up last night.

And if he really was in danger every second at Fairview, why turn up there at all? And who was he in danger from? Artie? Artie's mum? The idea was laughable.

But who else?

The police.

The idea just popped into my head. Then I remembered something Artie had told me. Mr Travers was 'unexpectedly back in Britain'.

UNEXPECTEDLY.

Was that a clue? What about if Mr Travers had committed a crime. A robbery maybe? He'd have had to leave France dead fast then, wouldn't he?

And now he was on the run and desperate to hide out somewhere for a few days, so he jumps at this job teaching Artie. That's why he turned up before he was expected.

But he couldn't stay long, not with police in two countries searching for him.

And he probably didn't work alone either. In fact, his fellow burglars will no doubt help Mr Travers escape to a safe place soon — on Friday night, maybe? But for now, he's just got to lie very low and hope he's not discovered. That's why he's in danger every second. It all seemed to fit.

So had I solved this case at a speed even Hercule Poirot would have envied?

And was I in the middle of a real-life mystery?

Chapter Seven

Fake Glasses

Next day, in the middle of double maths, I was struck by a horrible thought. If Mr Travers was on the run, how safe were Artie and his mum? And shouldn't I at least warn them?

But what on earth could I say? "Hi folks, just popped round to tell you that I believe your new tutor has, in fact, turned to crime and is now using your home as a temporary hide out. I have absolutely no evidence for saying this at all." And I really didn't. There was nothing remotely suspicious about Mr Travers – except for his thoughts.

Later, when I went into the library, Lucy – yes, Lucy – smiled at me. "I just had to talk to you about the ending of *The ABC Murders*." Her eyes were positively shining.

"It's mint, isn't it?" I said.

"And so ingenious ..." She stopped. A gang of girls had marched into the library and were making straight for us.

"Oh, do carry on with your very interesting conversation," said Nicola. "That's if we are allowed to breathe the same air as you, Lucy."

Lucy fled.

"Why don't you all go and freeze your teeth," I muttered. A fairly lame insult and I didn't exactly shout it either. I was angry with the girls from my class, but I was also embarrassed that I'd been caught conversing with the most unpopular girl in the school.

And then I was annoyed with myself for being embarrassed. So yeah, I was pretty mixed up. Anyway, I didn't see Lucy until History when I overheard:

I mustn't do anything except sit here

like a tortoise with its head tucked right inside its shell. I actually peeked my head out to talk to Matt and ... it's just not worth it. Anyway, I'm sure Matt thinks I'm a freak like everyone else does.

Right then I wanted to shout across the classroom, "Lucy, I so don't! And why shouldn't you speak in lessons?"

Today, Mr Rickets, the history teacher, was giving one of his famous quizzes. After a shaky start, he's now one of our favourite teachers. He can be quite funny too.

Today, he placed one Christmas cracker on the table. "This is a very early Christmas present for one lucky person. I know. How generous am I? It's a prize for today's star student."

Everyone pretended to be excited, and then he was off firing questions about the reign of Queen Elizabeth I. Lucy answered every question correctly – inside her head. But she didn't say one answer aloud. She didn't dare. So in the end, I stuck up my hand and borrowed a couple of her answers.

"You are working well today, Matt."

"Just call me the boy with two brains." I grinned. I thought this might stir Lucy into speaking. But it didn't.

Finally, Mr Rickets turned to Lucy. "Why don't you tell everyone when Queen Elizabeth's reign ended?"

Right away I overheard her think *1603*, but to Mr Rickets she only said, "Sorry, I don't know."

I really hated to see Lucy just opting out of everything.

Mr Rickets turned to me. "Can you help Lucy out?"

"Is it 1603?" I said.

Mr Rickets was so chuffed, he presented me with the Christmas cracker.

"May I just say this is probably the proudest moment of my life," I grinned.

Then at the end of the lesson, I marched up to Lucy. "You knew every one of those answers, didn't you?"

An uneasy look came over her face. "Well, er ..."

"Of course you did, so this cracker is yours

really, although I'm keeping it." Half the class was watching me, but you know what, I couldn't have cared less. I was too worked up. It wasn't right that Lucy was afraid to speak.

"And don't allow other people to intimidate you and just sit there like a dead tortoise," I said, "because you're worth all of them put together. And, by the way, I don't think you're weird at all." Lucy's eyes were popping out of her head now. "In fact, I like you. And here are the Agatha Christie books I promised. Bye."

Emma, who'd been part of the audience to this scene, rushed up to me. "Did you just say you liked Lucy Chu?"

"I did," I said loudly, defiantly.

"But she totally loves herself," said Emma.

I shook my head. "She so doesn't and you'd see that if you gave her a chance."

I felt proud of myself standing up for Lucy until I wondered – without my crystal, would I have realised Lucy was completely different to her image?

To be honest, probably not, and I'm sure I would have gone along with everyone else.

But my crystal had shown me there's more to everyone than you might imagine — which brought me back to Mr Travers.

As soon as I got home, I decided to google him. Only when I started typing I realised I hadn't a clue what his first name was. So instead I tried 'Mr Travers, tutor for children'.

And I did find something. He was with an agency that had a picture of him in those grizzly glasses (they surely deserved a web page all of their own), and a bit about him. His first name was Sam. He was 31 and had been incredibly busy, as there was a list of all his jobs, including that one in Paris.

It was the last one listed. There was no mention of his sudden departure. I didn't have an address for the French family. Should I try to track them down and ask a few questions about why he left so abruptly? I wasn't quite sure how to go about that. And, to be honest, I was a bit dazzled by all those reviews. No one had a bad word to say about him. He was 'brilliantly dedicated', 'inspiring' and even a 'miracle worker'. Yes, someone actually called him that.

But now, overnight, he'd transformed himself into a criminal who had to flee back to Britain. My theory seemed less and less likely. Maybe there was some incredibly boring reason for him 'being in danger every second at Fairview'.

Maybe.

And then Artie invited Scampi and me round for our tea. At first, I only saw Mr Travers very briefly. He bounced into the sitting room just after I'd arrived, gave me a broad smile and said, "Hey, good to see you again and you too, Scampi, of course. Might catch you both later." Then he went out.

"Where's he gone off to?" I asked.

Artie shrugged. "He often goes off around now, probably has a drink in a pub somewhere. He needs it, teaching me all day."

Was that really where Mr Travers had gone?

"Still, he must be a great tutor," said Artie.

"Why?" I asked.

"Well it feels as if we're not doing any work at all, just chatting, which is brilliant really."

'Brilliant' — that was the word used over and over to describe Mr Travers' teaching style. He had such a lucrative career too. Could he really have given it all up for a life of crime?

Then I forgot about Mr Travers for a bit. I was too busy showing off, letting Artie see all the tricks I'd taught Scampi. "Come. Sit. Fetch. Roll over …"

"I'm massively impressed," said Artie, when we'd finished. "Now on YouTube, I watched this woman teach her dog to high five. You get him to sit, then gently tap one of his feet …"

We were so intent on teaching Scampi this vital new skill we didn't hear Mr Travers return. He stood in the doorway smiling at us. "So now it's Scampi's turn to get some coaching."

"And he's much cleverer than me," said Archie excitedly. "Watch this."

Mr Travers sat back in the chair he always occupied and watched Scampi perform all his tricks once more. Only this time, I let Artie issue all the commands. I noticed how Mr Travers had whipped his glasses off and looked suddenly very tired. I edged my crystal towards him and overheard:

I don't know how people can wear glasses all day. They feel so very heavy and uncomfortable.

That was a bit odd. I mean, he's had to wear glasses for yonks, hasn't he? He was certainly wearing them in that picture taken of him two or three years ago.

Scampi had just finished his act – to loud applause from Mr Travers – when Artie's mum wandered in.

"Mum, you should see all the tricks Scampi can do …" began Artie.

"I'm looking forward to doing exactly that later," she cooed. "Artie, you haven't seen where I put my bracelet, have you?"

"You've got so many bracelets," he replied.

"This was the diamond one. The clasp needed repairing."

"Don't remember," said Artie. "Much more important, have you found the tickets for the panto on Friday night?"

She considered for a moment. "Yes I have, they were in my handbag all the time."

"What do you bet your bracelet is in there somewhere too?" said Artie.

His mum turned to Mr Travers. "I was going to make you some coffee, but I'm still not sure exactly how you like it. Was it—?"

"Don't worry," interrupted Mr Travers, jumping up. "I'll make the drinks."

"That's so kind of you. I'm having one of my absent-minded days," she added as they left together.

I noticed Mr Travers had left his glasses behind. And on impulse, I bolted across the room and picked them up. They looked even thicker close-up. Next, I tried the glasses on.

Artie laughed. "I bet you can't see a single thing can you?" He raised his hand. "How many fingers am I holding up?"

"Three," I said at once.

"Very good."

"Not really. Do you want to hear something strange?"

"Always," replied Artie.

"I can see through these glasses perfectly."

Chapter Eight

An Impostor

"I'm certain," I went on, "these are just ordinary glasses. Here, you try them on."

Artie sprang up, but before he could grab them a voice from the doorway declared, "I knew I was missing something." And Mr Travers practically snatched his glasses from me. "Ah, that's better," he said, as he put them on again.

"Matt was saying that he could see through them perfectly," said Artie. "And he reckons they've just got ordinary glass in them."

I reddened, but Mr Travers didn't miss a beat as he said confidently, "Ah, I can see why they might seem like that, but actually, they're specially made for me, as I have this stigmatism in both eyes and they correct my vision for me."

"Wish I hadn't asked," yawned Artie.

"By the way, boys, I meant to say, I really think you should enter Scampi for competitions."

"That's actually a really good idea," said Artie, all interested now.

"I do have them occasionally." Mr Travers grinned. "And I wouldn't be surprised if Scampi won every prize going."

After he'd left, I immediately asked Artie, "Do you believe him?"

"I really do. Scampi is so—"

"I mean about his glasses," I interrupted.

Artie looked puzzled. "It was boring enough to be true. And why should he lie about it unless he thinks those glasses make him look less ugly." He grinned. "Hey, maybe you should get a pair."

"All right, Captain Sarcastic."

"Who cares anyway?" said Artie. "But you'll be doing me a huge favour if you let me help you train Scampi. You can keep all the prize money, of course."

"No way," I replied at once.

Artie leapt up. "Scampi's so bright we could teach him anything. Hey, Scampi, how would you like to learn how to moonwalk?"

Scampi, hearing his name, thumped his tail enthusiastically.

"There you go," yelled Artie. "Scampi wants to moonwalk."

"You're mad," I laughed. I knew one thing for certain – with Artie, I'd made a new mate.

A warm glow enveloped me until I thought again about those glasses. Was Mr Travers telling the truth?

Or was it my first real clue? And how about what my crystal had picked up:

I don't know how people can wear glasses all day.

You would think he'd only just started wearing them. But I knew that wasn't true. So why was he thinking that?

No wonder my head was spinning. And it was still spinning the next day when I saw something else incredible. Emma and Lucy were walking down the corridor together, deep in conversation.

Later, Emma sped up to me. "How did you know?"

I raised an enquiring eyebrow.

"Lucy isn't stuck up at all – just very, very shy. I really shouldn't have gone along with what everyone said. Well, everyone except you. So, I repeat, how did you know?"

It was all because of my crystal, of course, but I couldn't say that. So I ducked the question and asked, "So what were you two nattering about?"

"You, mainly."

"Top subject."

"She thinks you're … funny."

"Every girl thinks I'm funny," I sighed. "Just as every girl likes me but only as a friend."

Emma gave me an odd look for a moment. "I don't know about that," she began. My heart started to thump. But then she continued, "Lucy said she's been up all night reading one of the books you loaned her, *Death on the Nile*, and wants to talk to you about it."

A couple of minutes later, Lucy did just that. She still chatted to my shoes rather than my face, and so quietly you had to strain to hear everything she said. But she was very, very excited.

"I love," she said, "trying to see if I can solve mysteries and work out what a clue means."

"So do I," agreed Emma.

"Well here's something to exercise your little grey cells then," I said suddenly. "Why should a guy wear glasses all the time – really thick ones too – that only contain ordinary glass?"

"Is this from a book?" asked Lucy.

I shook my head.

"So you know someone like that?" asked Emma.

"Just answer my question," I persisted.

"To make himself look more intellectual," began Emma.

"Or he could be in disguise," suggested Lucy.

"No, he's worn these glasses for yonks," I said.

"So he is a real person then," cried Emma.

"Maybe he's a secret agent," suggested Lucy. "And these glasses are the way he receives special messages."

Then the bell rang. History again. I turned to Lucy. "When Rickets asks a question today and you know the answer, stick your hand up."

"But only if you want to," said Emma at once. "Stop being so bossy, Matt."

Lucy just smiled faintly. But in history, she answered one question correctly – after Rickets had asked her to speak up. And then there was no stopping her. It was incredible. She knew absolutely everything – probably more than Rickets. I felt like applauding.

"I got a bit carried away," Lucy muttered to me afterwards. "I said too much, didn't I?"

"No, you were awesome."

She then added, "I've thought of another reason why your guy might wear fake glasses."

I smiled. "Go on then."

"What about if he's disguising himself as someone who needs to wear glasses?" Lucy's eyes opened very wide. "It would make it much more exciting if he's an impostor, wouldn't it?"

Chapter Nine

Trailing Mr Travers

All the way home my mind was racing.

Of course, Lucy's idea was totally incredible.

For a start, if this Mr Travers was a fake – well where was the real one? Could he be imprisoned somewhere – locked away in a cellar maybe – his hands and feet tied, a gag in his mouth, desperate to be rescued?

Then I grinned. This was becoming more and more unlikely. Anyway, why should this impostor – if that's what he was – go to so much trouble? And why on earth should he want to pretend to be Artie's tutor?

I searched and searched my mind but I couldn't find a single reason.

Even so, there was something sinister about Mr Travers. Or was there? If I didn't have my crystal and had only met him at Artie's house, I wouldn't have given him a second thought. Even the glasses, which weren't really glasses, wouldn't have bothered me. I might have thought it was a bit odd – eccentric, even – but nothing more. And that was still the only clue I had.

Then I had an idea. Artie mentioned how Mr Travers often went off for a walk around five o'clock. So how about if Scampi and me followed him?

That night the grass had a coating of frost already. It was absolutely freezing. I decided I greatly preferred trailing people in the summer. We nearly came back.

But we didn't, and just before five o'clock Scampi and I waited, shivering under the branches of a large oak tree, near Artie's house. Scampi gave such a sad little whimper. "I know it's cold," I said. "Look, we'll give him until—"

A little shudder ran through me.

I'd just spotted a tall, bespectacled figure moving briskly in our direction.

"Stay still," I whispered to Scampi. The branches rustled in the sharp wind as Mr Travers came past us. All of a sudden, I forgot about being bitterly cold, and felt like a proper detective on the trail of – well, what was I about to discover?

Mr Travers was certainly moving at quite a pace. We had to walk fast to keep him in sight. He quickly reached the parade of shops. Then quite unexpectedly, he looked round as if he had heard something. Scampi and I swerved into a shop doorway.

We waited, holding our breath. Or rather, I did. Scampi was looking more than a bit puzzled, uncertain if he liked this new game.

Then we sneaked a glance – Mr Travers had reached the end of the road and was going on to the one shop I never visited – a very large, and I'm sure very boring, supermarket. Surely he wasn't going to just do a bit of shopping. That would be such an anticlimax.

But no – he was making for the car park at the back of the supermarket. Some cars were still there, but right then not a single human, except for Mr Travers who was striding across it. Scampi and I hovered by the supermarket exit, where all the trolleys were kept.

Mr Travers stopped beside a black car. The driver – who I couldn't really see – wound down the window, then Mr Travers said something and took out of his pocket a very small parcel.

Did I dare take a closer look? Yes I did.

We sidled closer, taking great care to stay under cover of the cars. I watched the driver snatch up Mr Travers' parcel, as if he had a right to it.

I wondered what Mr Travers had given him? And why meet him here in an empty car park? That was dead suspicious.

Suddenly, it hit me. I knew what might be in that little parcel.

The bracelet Artie's mum had lost.

Well, it was possible – wasn't it? Artie's mum had left it lying around. So Mr Travers nicked it and was now passing it on to this dodgy-looking guy in the car.

If only I could hear what they were saying. "Come on," I whispered to Scampi. We carefully edged our way even closer, Scampi sniffing me eagerly. He liked it when I was crouched down to his size. I caught Mr Travers say snappily, "No, you're not dragging this out any longer. I go tomorrow night with whatever I'm able to get."

This was fantastic. I was finding out so much.

And then it happened.

My nose began twitching. And the very next second an ear-splitting *WWWWACHOOO* just erupted across the car park. I tell you, it was loud enough to drown out a pneumatic drill! (And also managed to decorate the boot of the car I was sheltering under!) Right away, just to add even more fun to the occasion, I immediately let rip with another *WWWACHOOO*.

Mr Travers jerked away from the car like a puppet whose strings had suddenly been cut. I could hear him breathing deeply as he started searching around the car park for the source of that highly mysterious sound effect.

I didn't want him to discover me hiding. So instead, I unfurled myself from my hiding place and as I got to my feet, said casually, "Hi there – isn't it chilly tonight?"

Mr Travers gaped at me and Scampi. "What on earth are you …?" he began.

"We thought we'd surprise you," I said, sounding about three, but it was all I could think of.

"And is Artie going to pop up now as well?" he asked.

"No, just us tonight," I grinned cheerily.

"Well, you've caught me—" he began.

"I certainly have—"

"Giving my mate his Christmas present. He's going away to Australia tomorrow, you see. Lucky or what?"

Mr Travers turned back to the guy in the car. He spoke very softly. The driver didn't say a single word in reply, not even "Happy Christmas" – just tore off at some speed.

Mr Travers loped over to us – his familiar smile back on his face. He started patting

Scampi while murmuring, "How are you then, boy? Enjoying your long walk?" Meanwhile, I'd set my crystal to work and overheard:

Somehow that punk's followed me here. But I don't think Artie sent him. He's acting alone. I sensed he was suspicious of me. I don't know why. But I'll make certain he doesn't do anything to stop tomorrow night.

Those last words were chilling all right. But do you know what made it far, far worse? All the time, Mr Travers carried on smiling and generally acting as if he was absolutely delighted to see me.

That's why I announced, "We've got to go."

For the first time, I was actually scared of Mr Travers.

He looked up, "I'm worried about you, Matt, out here on your own. I think I should walk you home."

That was the very last thing I wanted. "I don't want to put you to all that trouble." I actually started backing away from him.

"It's no trouble at all."

And then two things happened. A family appeared, laden down with shopping and all chattering away. And my mobile rang. I answered it immediately.

It was my mum, demanding to know why I wasn't home yet for my tea. She sounded absolutely furious. And I'd never been so pleased to hear her in my life!

"Sorry, Mum, but I've just been chatting with Artie's tutor."

Mr Travers actually froze.

"Yeah, OK, Mum. Bye. See you soon."

I turned to Mr Travers. "Would you believe Mum is insisting she picks me up."

That was a lie, actually. Mum just told me to be home in five minutes or my tea would be thrown away.

"Well, look after yourself, won't you?" Mr Travers' voice oozed concern.

"I will," I replied firmly.

"Great to see you," I added. I could be just as fake as him. Then Scampi and I tore off.

At home, Mum and Dad joined forces to give me a truly massive lecture about how important it was to be on time for meals and how I'd be grounded until I was ninety if I was ever a millisecond late again. It cheered me up, actually. It made everything seem so normal – until later, when I was in bed.

I couldn't stop replaying the last words I'd overheard:

But I'll make certain he doesn't do anything to stop tomorrow night.

Mr Travers wasn't just a phoney. He was a highly dangerous phoney.

Then I wondered why the urgency? Why did this plan have to take place on Friday night?

Why not Saturday night or ...?

I shot up in bed.

Of course! Of course!

Neither Artie nor his mum had ever met the genuine Mr Travers. But Artie's dad had. So he'd spot this wasn't the real tutor right away. There'd be no fooling him.

And Artie's dad comes home on Saturday.

That would explain the rush. And I knew I couldn't hang about either. Straight after school tomorrow, I'd warn both Artie and his mum.

But what could I say to them? I still didn't have much proof. I could mention Mr Travers' meeting in the car park. But he'd have an explanation for that.

There was one other way – TELL THEM ABOUT MY CRYSTAL.

I'd have to break it to them gently, of course, say something like, "Guess what, folks, I have a superpower." Next, I'd give them a demonstration or two. Artie would be so impressed. I'd enjoy telling them actually. And then they'd believe every word I told them.

Only Mrs Jameson had said – in a letter she'd left for me – no one else must discover my crystal's secret.

But wasn't this an exception? A total emergency? I was sure it was. If only Mrs Jameson were here to advise me. Sometimes, when I'm holding the crystal, I feel oddly close to her. As if she's not very far away at all, but hovering, unseen, close by me.

So right then, I took hold of my crystal and whispered to Mrs Jameson to help me and somehow tell me what to do. I held it tightly for ages and ages. I don't exactly know what I was expecting. But absolutely nothing happened.

Of course, the idea of Mrs Jameson being nearby was only a comforting illusion.

Really, I was totally on my own.

Chapter Ten

Ghostly Warning

"Quiet, everyone. This is important," announced Miss Shah, clapping her hands at the end of registration. "Has anyone seen Lucy today?"

The question crashed into my thoughts about what I was going to do after school — I'd already invited myself and Scampi round to Artie's for an early tea.

"So no one has seen Lucy today?" repeated Miss Shah, staring round at the blank faces anxiously. Then I heard the school secretary, who was standing beside her, whisper, "Her parents insist Lucy left for school as usual today – but they noticed she hadn't taken the homework she was doing last night. So this is very puzzling."

It certainly was. Where could Lucy be?

As we left for our first lesson, I asked Emma, "You don't suppose Lucy has actually run away do you?"

"I wouldn't be surprised," she replied glumly. "When I spoke to her last night she was dead upset."

"About what?"

"Haven't you heard?" she asked.

"Heard what?"

"Some of our lovely classmates have been posting pictures of Lucy and saying stuff like, 'This is what a saddo freak looks like'."

I shook my head in disbelief. "But why are they being so nasty?"

"They've decided Lucy was showing off in history yesterday – and it 'offended' them."

"You're joking," I began.

Emma lowered her voice. "The awful thing is, it's happened to Lucy before – at her old school. In fact, people were putting up horrible comments and pictures about her every night. That's why she left and why she was terrified of drawing attention to herself here. Last night she said to me, 'I'm just a freak, aren't I?' "

I could feel a lump in my throat. And neither of us spoke for a moment until I said, "Tonight, we'll have to go round to see Lucy, prove to her she's got mates now."

"A brilliant idea," said Emma. So we arranged to meet up at half past seven.

After school, I walked home on my own as Emma was Christmas shopping with her mum.

Every shop was busy trying to lure customers in with incredible price reductions. The coffee shop on the corner was even offering a free homemade mince pie with every drink. I'd have loved to have sampled one of those. But I had no time. Instead I needed to dash home, grab Scampi and then tear off to Artie's house. I waited impatiently for the traffic lights to change colour. I edged to the front, crowds were jostling round me. Then I stopped abruptly.

The oddest thing had started happening. My crystal was warming up all by itself. But that was impossible. I had to hold the crystal to activate it. That was the way it worked. Yet I could feel it against my belt, fizzing with heat. And it seemed to be urging me to pick it up.

So I grabbed it, my heart beating wildly. My crystal was scorching hot and I could only grasp it long enough to pick up a voice that was very faint, as if someone were whispering to me from the bottom of a deep well. The words crept into my head:

YOU ARE IN GREAT DANGER, WATCH OUT!

I couldn't hold the crystal any longer. The very next second, I felt a strong push in my back. It was propelling me into the path of a car swishing past.

Without the crystal's warning, I'd have been right under the wheels of that car. But alerted, I somehow managed to twist away from it and hurl myself backwards, flinging my arms out as I fell to the ground. For a moment, all I could see was a blur of feet.

The lights must have changed colour but

everyone was milling around me. I was helped to my feet and I was even brushed down. A woman, her face white with shock, shouted, "Whatever were you playing at?" While a smartly-dressed man observed, "There could have been a nasty accident." I smiled grimly at that one.

A bottle of water made its way to me. I gulped down a few drops. "Can you walk?" asked someone else. I nodded. I felt shaky and my legs were a bit sore but it could have been so much worse. And then, elbowing their way through the crowd came Emma and her mum.

"Matt, are you all right?" cried Emma.

I forced a smile. "Never better."

Someone else was telling Emma's mum, "That boy was rushing about and lost his balance."

"We'll get you home, love," said Emma's mum. Half holding on to Emma, I tottered off to their car. An hour later, my mum was still saying I should be in bed. We compromised, with me lying on the couch in the sitting room.

I was still in a daze, especially over that warning from my crystal. Had it come from

Mrs Jameson? That was my first thought. And second, it didn't sound like her voice. But then it didn't sound like anyone's voice, it was too faint and far away. A ghostly whisper ... well maybe. Anyway, it was a mystery I couldn't fathom right now.

But there was no mystery about who had so nearly pushed me under that car. It had to be Mr Travers. I never saw him, of course, so I didn't have a scrap of evidence.

Mum had already rung Artie's mum to say I was recovering from an accident and couldn't go round as planned. Then Mum took my mobile away, saying I needed complete rest. So I wasn't able to even call Artie.

But I couldn't leave Artie and his mum at the mercy of Mr Travers. Still, Emma was coming back. I'd have to try to explain to her what I thought had really happened.

If only I had some proof.

The doorbell rang. And Mum brought in ... Lucy.

That gave me a jolt.

"Another friend has heard about your

accident," announced Mum, "and wanted to see how you are. Would you like a drink, er …?"

"Lucy – and no, thank you."

After Mum had gone, Scampi strolled over to investigate the newcomer. Lucy smiled down at him.

"Where on earth have you been?"

Still staring hard at Scampi, she said quietly, "Nothing very original. Most of the day I was hiding in the coffee shop."

I sat up. "Not the one on the corner by the traffic lights."

"That's the one." And then Lucy slowly looked up at me. "I saw the accident, Matt – and I saw the man you told us about – the one with the very thick glasses."

Chapter Eleven

Toppling a Supervillain

This could change everything.

"Tell me exactly what you saw, Lucy," I said, adding kindly, "Sit down first though – and make yourself at home."

Lucy sat on the edge of the hardest chair in the room. She looked dead nervous – but excited as well. "I was staring idly out of the coffee shop window – something I'd been doing for hours – when I saw you waiting to cross the road. And a bit later, there was the man exactly as you'd described him. I remember thinking how you hadn't exaggerated about those glasses. They really are incredibly thick. And then I noticed him edging closer and closer to you. But he didn't talk to you, did he?"

"Not a word, I never even realised he was there … although I guessed."

"And then I saw you fall over."

"Well, actually …" I began. "No, later, carry on."

"I sped out of the coffee shop, ready to help you. But Emma and her mum went over to you, so I realised I wasn't needed. And then I spotted the man with the big glasses again. I was very surprised he didn't wait to see if you were all right. Instead, he just slipped quietly away. I thought that was very odd."

"Not really, you see, he'd just tried to push me in front of a speeding car."

Lucy didn't look as astonished as I'd expected – mildly surprised was more like it. Then her eyes actually shone as she said, with the air of someone who had just solved a puzzle, "I knew there was something highly suspicious about—" she stopped. Dad was hovering in the doorway with Emma.

He gave me a goofy grin. "You certainly are popular tonight."

After he'd left, Emma demanded, "Lucy, why didn't you answer any of my texts? I've been so worried."

"I know, and I'm sorry," muttered Lucy.

"Where have you been then?" Emma still sounded indignant and a bit hurt.

So I chipped in, "Lucy's been in the local coffee shop and very lucky for me that she was."

"Why?" asked Emma.

"Because she saw someone try to shove me in front of a car."

"What?" cried Emma.

"I couldn't tell you before, but someone pushed me hard in the back when that car was going past. I was certain it was Mr Travers but I had no proof. Only Lucy saw him hovering behind me, just before the accident and then disappear pretty swiftly straight afterwards."

"But why would he do something so terrible?" Emma cried, sitting down on the couch beside me.

"Let me explain," I said, adding, "I don't

want my parents to know about any of this yet — so keep your voices down."

I told them everything — except, of course, what I'd overheard from the crystal.

"So you really believe," said Emma slowly, "Mr Travers is an impostor? And you saw him handing over a stolen bracelet to an associate last night?"

"And that's just the start, isn't it?" cut in Lucy. "The big robbery will be tonight when Artie and his mum are out of the house."

"You're exactly right," I said.

"And when Artie and his mum come back," continued Lucy, "their house will have been ransacked by the fake tutor who, of course, will have disappeared too." She turned to me. "What time did you say Artie and his mum were leaving?"

"About seven o'clock."

Lucy sprang to her feet. "Well, we haven't a moment to lose."

Emma, not to be outdone, jumped up too and then helped me up.

"If Mum drives us, we'll be there in no time,"

I said.

But that was a massive if.

And Mum wasn't at all happy about me going out. She said I just wasn't well enough. I told her I felt much better (and I did – sort of).

"We'll take really, really good care of him," said Emma, taking one of my arms.

"We certainly will," agreed Lucy who, to my great surprise, then clutched my other arm.

And Mum actually smiled.

"Plus I'll be taking Scampi as well." Scampi's ears shot up at the mention of his name. "So that's a whole team of bodyguards."

In the end, Mum very reluctantly agreed. On the condition, though, that I only stayed for half an hour.

"You couldn't make it an hour, could you?" I asked.

"Half an hour or nothing," said Mum firmly.

"We'll just have to talk fast to Artie and his Mum," I murmured to Lucy.

"Don't worry," replied Lucy, "I won't let you down. I'll tell them exactly what I saw."

I sent Artie a quick text to say we were on

our way — and be sure to wait for us.

Just as we were getting ready to leave, Mum's mobile went off. And in the end it was Dad who drove us, with Lucy in the front, Emma, Scampi and me in the back.

At exactly a quarter to seven, Dad pulled up outside Artie's house. As I got out of the car, I winced. A sharp pain ran through my leg.

"Take it easy, Matt," called Dad through the window. "And look after him, girls." He added, "I'll be back in exactly thirty minutes."

I rang impatiently on the doorbell — twice. And several seconds later, twice again. Not a sound, and no lights, apart from the security one.

"Do you suppose everyone really is out?" asked Emma.

"Artie and his mum weren't leaving until seven," I said.

"And anyway, Artie will have got my text saying I had to see him urgently. They're in that house and so is, well let's call him Super Fake. No, something's happened."

Now, my crystal can't eavesdrop through

walls – but it can through glass. So I hobbled off – my leg was really starting to play up again – and pretended to be peering through a heavily curtained window, when actually, I was activating my crystal. Very soon I picked up Super Fake:

That wretched kid again. I'll just stay quiet – there's absolutely no way I can let him in now.

Well, I wasn't going anywhere after that. So I yelled through the letterbox. "Mr Travers, I know you're in there. And I'm not leaving until you answer the door." As if to back me up, Scampi started to howl. "Mr Travers!" I thundered so loudly, the people opposite started peeping through their windows. "Mr Travers, open up now!"

"Yeah, come on, show yourself!" yelled Lucy so angrily Emma actually stepped back from her. Suddenly, quite unexpectedly, the door opened a crack. And there was Mr Travers, squinting at us.

"I'm very sorry, guys, to keep you waiting." His hair was dishevelled and he was speaking very softly. "But I've got a really awful migraine. And when that happens, I just have to lie in the dark for — well, two or three hours sometimes. As for Artie — I'm afraid he and his mother have gone. They were worried about the Friday night traffic, I think. You've only just missed them."

I had to marvel at how plausible he sounded. But I was certain what he said about Artie and his mum was a big fat lie. Then I darted a glance at Lucy, just to completely confirm he was the guy she'd seen from the coffee shop. She nodded slowly, grimly.

"Actually, it was you we really wanted to talk to," I said.

"Me, really, that's very flattering. But I'm sorry, I'm in no state to talk to anyone now."

"It's very important," said Lucy suddenly.

He looked with surprise at her, but then said extremely politely, "Well, come back tomorrow morning. How about that?" When, of course, he knew he'd be far away from here. He started to close the door.

I had to think extremely fast. So I started gabbling something about a message I wanted to leave for Artie. Total gibberish, but I needed to keep him there while I used my crystal – which fortunately was still hot – to talk to Scampi.

"Run about now, Scampi," I urged, nodding towards the half-open door. I repeated the message again. "Run around now." And then accidentally-on-purpose I let go of Scampi's lead.

At once, Scampi barrelled past Super Fake and, yelping happily, pounded up the stairs. I think he loved tearing round houses even more than racing about in the park.

Mr Travers just stood there, he couldn't believe what had just happened. Neither, actually, could Emma and Lucy.

"I'm very sorry," I said. "I'll have to come in and get Scampi or he'll never come downstairs."

Mr Travers's face twisted with frustration. "Well, hurry up."

I stumbled inside while Mr Travers closed the door very firmly on Emma and Lucy. "Sorry, but I can't let anyone else in."

"Be careful, Matt, he's dangerous," yelled Lucy after me.

Mr Travers heard this and for the first time that confident smile actually flickered. "How on earth am I dangerous? What game are you all playing?"

I looked him straight in the eye. "Lucy watched you trying to push me in front of a car this afternoon."

At once, Mr Travers stood very still. He had a weird pent-up look, as if he were holding his breath. "That is total fantasy. Why on earth should I do something—"

"Because I know too much," I interrupted.

"I shall be delighted to listen to all your wild imaginings tomorrow when I'm feeling better. I think I have been remarkably patient, but my patience is now at an end so please collect your dog and go!"

He was trying very hard to stay in control. But his voice was suddenly shrill and angry. His mask was slipping and he was rapidly morphing into the desperate guy I'd overheard last Sunday night.

Scampi pounded down the stairs, his lead tripping after him. I was still instructing him via my crystal to run around, so he tore past us and started enthusiastically exploring downstairs.

"Get that dog and leave." Mr Travers's voice was actually cracking.

"That dog is called Scampi, as you well know," I said. "And he's only being friendly."

But then I noticed something very odd. Scampi had stopped charging about and instead was pawing away at one of the rooms.

"What is it?" I asked, moving towards him. Scampi became more and more excited, just as if someone he knew and really liked was ...

I pointed my crystal at the room.

And then a shiver spread across my skin. My crystal overheard:

Got to wake up and call for help. Must try very hard.

I choked off a cry.

It was Artie. Only he sounded very odd, as if he'd been drugged. My heart beating furiously,

I tried the handle, with Scampi eagerly sniffing beside me.

It was locked.

"Why's the door locked?" I demanded, feeling suddenly as if I were in a crazy kind of dream.

"Mrs Prentice locked it before she left."

"No she didn't. Open it up!" I yelled.

"I don't have the key and why on earth would you—"

"Because Artie's in there. What have you done to him?

Mr Travers gave a short laugh that had no humour in it.

The doorbell rang and Emma shouted through the letterbox. "Are you all right, Matt?"

"I suggest you both go and join your friends immediately," said Mr Travers, marching into the large hall and about to open the front door.

"I know you're not the real Mr Travers," I called.

That stopped him all right. He whirled round. "When I tell Mrs Prentice about your extraordinary behaviour tonight she will not be happy. In fact, she may well ban you from visiting here again. Would you like that? Go now and I shan't mention tonight. Is that a deal?" His voice was shaking all over the place, while my crystal picked up:

My cousin's in France, and he can't have contacted anyone, certainly not this little punk. He's bluffing – he's got to be.

Once again my crystal had delivered the goods.

Limping only slightly, I began walking triumphantly towards him with Scampi right beside me, panting excitedly. "I know the real Mr Travers," I announced, "is far away in France."

His eyes wild with shock, Super Fake tried to speak, but no words came out.

"And you," I yelled, "are, in fact ..." I paused and jabbed my last two words at him, "... his cousin!"

The effect of the last two words was so magical I could only watch open-mouthed as Super Fake let out a strange gurgled cry and then toppled on to the carpet.

I leant over him to just check he hadn't died of shock. He hadn't. He'd only fainted.

The doorbell started to ring insistently. I stepped over him to answer it.

Emma and Lucy fell inside as I announced, "We've got to phone the police and my parents. Artie and his mum are still here – but they've been drugged so we need to find a key to—"

I stopped, both girls were gaping at Super Fake and then looking up at me as if they'd never seen me before.

"He's … he's …" gasped Emma.

"He's certainly not in peak health right now," I said.

"Matt, you've flattened him," spluttered Emma, shaking her head in wonder.

"But how?" asked Lucy.

I smiled highly mysteriously. "Let's just say, I have my methods."

Chapter Twelve

Final Surprise

"As Hercule Poirot himself might say," — I grinned around at everyone — "this has been one of the most interesting cases I have ever come across."

It was half past three on Saturday afternoon. Outside, the rain was pouring down and it was freezing cold. But inside my sitting room there was a bright fire and so many people that Mum needed to bring in extra chairs to seat everyone.

As well as my parents and Alison, Artie was here with his mum and dad (who'd flown back several hours early from Germany), and seated alongside me were Emma and Lucy, with Scampi lying by my feet.

And the room was abuzz with anticipation as I slowly got to my feet.

"Well, I've just come off the phone from the police who have been updating me," I began.

"Will you listen to him," scoffed Alison.

Poirot was very lucky he didn't have a sister.

"I bet the police congratulated you," said Artie, now his normal self again. "As you were suspicious of my phoney tutor from the start, weren't you?"

"After the fake glasses I was, but I couldn't think of a motive. Why on earth would he want to pretend to be your tutor?"

"Why indeed?" murmured Artie's dad dryly.

"Well, the police have filled me in on that one. Mr Travers — and by the way that was his real name — Ed Travers he's called. But it is his cousin, Sam, who is the tutor. Ed Travers was in fact an actor, still waiting for a lucky break. He was also in a real hole for money. He'd allowed his gambling debts to build alarmingly. And now they'd been sold on to a very tough gang who demanded payment at once.

"Ed Travers was in a very desperate situation. Then he heard that his highly successful cousin was back in Britain for a few days to talk at a conference. Borrowing money from his cousin really was his very last hope." I took a quick swig of water. All eyes – even Alison's – were locked on to me.

"Ed Travers found out where his cousin was staying. But he was too late. His cousin was already back on the plane to France. It seemed as if Ed Travers was out of luck again until, at the hotel, a boy on reception confused Ed with his cousin – they look very alike – and handed him a letter. It was from Artie's dad, who thought Mr Travers had come back to Britain for good and was offering him a job over the Christmas holidays."

The room had become absolutely still. I leaned forward. "So that's when Ed Travers hatched his wild and reckless scheme. He soon found out that Artie's family were very wealthy. Could he worm his way into the house as a tutor, find out what was worth stealing – and use that to pay off his debts? It was his very, very last chance. He had to move fast, though – as Artie's father knew the real Mr Travers and was due home on Saturday. Now, the two cousins were very similar, except Ed Travers was a bit taller and had perfect eyesight. So to complete the transformation he needed—"

"Phoney glasses," cut in Artie.

"I still can't believe," interrupted Artie's dad, "that when this … this criminal turned up at my home, no one thought to ask him for any proof of identity." Artie's dad, a small, wiry man with enormous black eyebrows turned to his wife.

"Well, as you knew him I thought I didn't need to check anything … and he came so early, and I was especially busy just then …" Her voice fell away.

"Don't forget, Dad," said Artie with one of his cheeky smiles, "you were the one who insisted I have a tutor. You could even say this is all your fault."

Before his dad could reply, Artie turned to me. "So when you followed Ed Travers you saw him handing over Mum's diamond bracelet?"

"Yeah, and that's when he totally freaked. He decided I had to be out of the way before the big robbery he'd planned for Friday night."

"What a very cruel man," said Mum.

"Anyway, when Ed Travers saw I was still mobile, he rushed his plan forward. He couldn't wait until Artie and his mum left for the panto. Instead, he put sleeping draughts in both their drinks. He planned to quickly raid the house of everything worth stealing, use this to pay off his huge debts and then flee the country."

"But instead we turned up," said Emma.

"And so lucky for us you did," said Artie's mum.

Emma said, "I still don't know exactly what you said to him, Matt, but by the time Lucy and I came in, Ed Travers was lying on the ground."

"Probably bored him to death," muttered Alison.

"I think it was the strain of it all," I said vaguely.

"By the time I arrived," said Dad, "he was a broken man, just sitting hunched in the corner. He didn't offer the police any resistance at all."

"Bit of an anticlimax really," I grinned. "He didn't have a criminal record and was very nervous about the whole operation. The police say he has already signed a full confession."

"May I say something now?" said Artie's dad, getting to his feet. I suspected he was far more used to talking than listening anyhow. "First of all, we are very, very grateful to you, young man."

"It wasn't only me," I said quickly. "Emma and Lucy were so smart and fearless—"

"Not forgetting Scampi," cut in Artie. Scampi wagged his tail on hearing his name.

"Well, thank you all for keeping my family safe," said Artie's dad. "And if ever, young man," he was looking fixedly at me now with his deep blue eyes, so exactly like Artie's, "I can do anything for you ..."

"Well, actually you can," I replied so promptly Mum gave a shocked gasp.

But Artie's dad said firmly, "Just name it, young man."

"Don't make Artie have another tutor," I said. "Or do any school work this holiday. Anyway, he's going to be extremely busy helping me to train Scampi."

Artie immediately declared, "Nice one, Matt!"

But Artie's dad's massive eyebrows shot up. "I wasn't expecting that."

"I know, but that's the favour you can do for me," I said quietly.

Artie's dad looked sharply at his son. "Do you promise to work much harder next term?"

Artie turned to his dad. "I really, really do."

"I don't believe a word of it," declared Artie's dad with a small smile. "But how can I refuse?" Then he swept out of the house, accompanied by his wife and a broadly grinning Artie. My mum and dad saw them off.

Alison shook her head at me and said very sarcastically, "Do let me know when the police offer you a job, won't you?"

After she'd gone, I asked, "Do you think I could swap my sister for a gerbil or something?"

I tuned to Lucy. "You know we couldn't have nailed Ed Travers without you."

"And you're not on your own any more,"

added Emma.

"You might want to be," I grinned, "but you're not, so see you on Monday, all right?"

"I've just helped to defeat a fake tutor," said Lucy slowly. "I still can't believe it." And for a moment she looked just as if she'd won the lottery. "So no, I'm not running away from anyone, and I'll be there on Monday all right."

Then it was only Emma left. "What are you up to tonight?" I asked.

"Going to have another look at Finn's shed."

"Lucky you," I said unenthusiastically.

"Well, he's got some amazing new gadgets I can't wait to see." My face dropped until Emma burst out laughing. "Great detective you are. Can't you tell a massive lie when you hear one?"

Still laughing, she suddenly hugged me, to my great surprise, before saying, "That night at Finn's – that awful night – you were going to ask me something weren't you?" Before I could reply she went on. "Well I hope you'll ask me again. Not here, not now, but later …"

After she'd gone, I asked Scampi, "Did that just happen? Did the only girl I've ever wanted to go out with, strongly hint ..."

I stopped. Dad was hovering.

"Yet another visitor for you."

A smartly dressed woman bustled in. For a moment I didn't recognise her. Then I did. It was Mrs Jameson's niece.

"I can only stay a minute, Matthew," she said. "But I thought I'd better deliver this personally. I found it among my aunt's belongings." She handed me an envelope with my name on it.

I opened it, with her standing right beside me, just as if we were about to announce the winners of an award together. "Now, I thought it might be a Christmas card," she went on, "and it is, but what a very odd message to write inside. Still, that's my aunt. She was rather eccentric, wasn't she?"

I didn't answer, I was still re-reading what Mrs Jameson had written to me. "Well, I thought you'd like to have it," Mrs Jameson's niece continued.

A smile slowly spread across my face. "This is amazing, thank you!" I gasped.

Looking distinctly puzzled by my enthusiasm,

Mrs Jameson's niece wished me a happy Christmas and left.

I just went on staring at Mrs Jameson's message.

To Matt,
Maybe I won't be as far away as you might think.

It wasn't an odd message at all. Maybe a bit eerie. But eerie in a totally brilliant, wonderful way.

For it means I've not only got a superpower, but a ghost is keeping an eye on me as well.

How lucky am I?

Anyway, I'm off now to ask Emma out. So yeah, you could say my story ends exactly as it began.

And don't forget, if you ever need my help, you don't need to say a single word, just send me a few thoughts …

I'll be listening.

About Pete Johnson

Pete's favourite subjects at school were English and history. His least favourite was maths.

He has always loved reading. When he was younger, Pete would read up to six books a week – even more in the school holidays!

His most favourite book as a child was *One Hundred and One Dalmatians*. He wrote to the author, Dodie Smith, and she encouraged him to become a writer.

Other childhood favourites include *The Witches* by Roald Dahl, *Tom's Midnight Garden* by Philippa Pearce and Enid Blyton's *The Mystery of the Invisible Thief*.

When he was younger, Pete used to sleepwalk. One night, he woke up in his pyjamas walking along a busy road.

He has a West Highland terrier called Hattie.

His favourite food is chocolate. He especially loves Easter eggs!

Pete loved to watch old black-and-white movies with his dad on Saturday night and used to review films on Radio 1. Sometimes he watched three films in a day! Pete has met lots of famous actors and collects signed film pictures.

He likes to start writing by eight o'clock in the morning. He reads all his books out loud to see if the dialogue sounds right. And if he's stuck for an idea, he goes for a long walk.

Wherever he goes, Pete always carries a notebook with him. "The best ideas come when you're least expecting them," he says. Why don't you try that too? Maybe you'll have a brilliant idea for your own book!

To find out more about Pete and his books, go to:

www.petejohnsonauthor.com

A Note from Pete

Books are dead until they are read. You have brought *MindReader: Ghostly Whisper* to life and I am most grateful to you.

Maybe now you'd like to talk about the story. A great way to do this is through a book club. Anyone can start one. So here are a few suggestions of what you might like to think about just to get going. (Of course you don't have to be in a book club – you can do it just for fun!)

Matt humiliated
- Matt is the hero of the story, yet in the first and second chapters we see him thoroughly humiliated. Did this surprise you?
- Did you laugh or feel sorry for Matt?
- Why do you think the book begins like this?

- Does it help us identify with Matt, showing that despite his superpower things can go wrong for him too?

"In danger every second" (*Chapter Three*)
- Matt is just 'surfing' when he picks up this thought. Were you as stunned as Matt by it?
- This is a highly unusual way to begin a mystery. Were you intrigued?
- If you had been Matt, would you have wanted to visit Fairview too? Why?

Lucy Chu — and not fitting in
- In Chapter Four we meet Lucy. What were your first impressions of her?
- How does your view of her change?
- Why don't the girls in Lucy's year like her? How fair are they being to Lucy?
- Think about a time when you didn't fit in and how that made you feel.
- Did you ever wish you were someone different or could change something about yourself?
- Discuss ways that people can learn to be more comfortable with their differences.

Matt and Emma

- Matt and Emma have an argument because Emma laughs at him (Chapter Two). Matt is shocked by her 'total disloyalty' and thinks she let him down. She says, "Well it was sort of funny." Who do you agree with? Is Matt over-reacting? Or should Emma have tried harder not to laugh?
- How serious an argument is it?
- What brings Matt and Emma back together (Chapter Four)?
- What advice would you give to someone who has an argument with a good friend?

Mystery stories and Agatha Christie

- As well as being a comedy and a school story this is also a mystery, with clues, suspects and danger. Were they your favourite parts of the story?
- Did you enjoy trying to solve the mystery?
- What other mystery books have you read?
- Have you ever read a book by Agatha Christie? Or watched a film or TV show based on her stories?

Matt's crystal

- How big a role does Matt's crystal play in the story?
- Would Matt have ever solved the mystery without it? Look at what he overhears in Chapters Seven and Nine, for instance.
- Look too at Chapter Ten. Does the crystal save Matt here?

Favourite character

- There are several contrasting characters in the story – Matt, Emma, Lucy, Artie and Finn. Did you have a favourite?
- Who are the most and least likeable?
- There is also, of course, Scampi. Could you guess the author is a dog lover?
- Matt feels he has made a new friend in Artie. Do you agree? Would you like Artie as a friend?
- Write the texts they might send each other when Artie returns to boarding school. Would Artie's texts be funny and full of jokes?
- Do you send texts? What sort of messages do you send?

Read all the MindReader adventures!

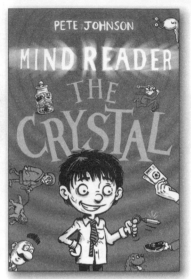 

978-1-78270-303-7 978-1-78270-304-4

Also by Pete Johnson…
Meet Louis the Laugh – the hilarious schoolboy
comedian with the world's worst parents!

  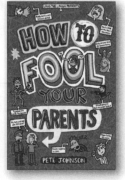

978-1-78270-160-6 978-1-78270-172-9 978-1-78270-247-4